Postman

GW00854963

The Breezy Day

Story by **John Cunliffe**
Pictures by **Celia Berridge**

from the original Television designs by Ivor Wood

Hippo

Scholastic Children's Books,
7-9 Pratt Street, London NW1 OAE UK
A division of Scholastic Publications Ltd
London - New York - Toronto - Sydney - Auckland

First published in hardback by André Deutsch Limited, 1985
This edition published in the UK by Scholastic Publications Ltd, 1995

Copyright © John Cunliffe, 1985
Illustrations copyright © Celia Berridge and Ivor Wood, 1985

ISBN 0 590 13258 X

All rights reserved
Printed by Mateu Cromo, S.A. Pinto (Madrid)

Typeset by Rapid

10 9 8 7 6 5 4 3 2 1

The right of John Cunliffe, Celia Berridge and Ivor Wood to
be identified as the author and illustrators of this work has
been asserted by them in accordance with the Copyright,
Designs and Patents Act, 1988.

This book is sold subject to the condition that it shall not, by way of trade
or otherwise be lent, resold, hired out, or otherwise circulated without the
publisher's prior consent in any form of binding other than that in
which it is published and without a similar condition, including this
condition, being imposed upon the subsequent purchaser.

It was a breezy day in Greendale. The leaves swirled about the road. The wind blew and buffeted Pat's van as he drove along the valley with the post.

"Hang on, Jess," he said, "it's a right job, driving in this wind."

A scrap of paper blew across his windscreen.

"Help I can't see!"

The wind was so strong that people could hardly stand up. They passed Alf Thompson along the road, and he was nearly blown off his feet. He had to hold his hat on with his stick.

Pat drove over the hill, and round a corner. He shouted, "LOOK OUT!" and stood on the brakes.

A tree had blown down, and fallen right across the road. Pat stopped just in time. He got out of the van to have a good look.

"How are we going to get past this lot?"

Jess came to have a look, too. He prowled along the fallen branches. He thought it made a lovely place to climb and play. Pat heard a voice.

"Hello, Pat!" It was Peter Fogg.

"This wretched wind!" said Peter. "Blowing trees down all over the place. Don't worry, Pat. I'll soon shift it. I'll nip down to the forestry place and borrow their lifting tackle. I won't be long!"

Pat went to have a look at the tree's roots. "No wonder it blew over," he said. "It's rotten."

Peter was soon back, on his tractor, with the lifting tackle. He had a big power-saw, too.

"Now then, we'll soon cut through this. Stand back," he said as he started the power-saw with a shattering roar, "these things don't half go."

He lopped the branches off, and Pat carried them into the field. Then Peter sliced the tree into pieces.

"Now then," he said, "let's see if wc can move it."

He backed the lifting tackle up to the tree. It was like a small crane. He fixed the chain round a piece of the trunk, and started the motor up. It lifted the heavy wood into the air.

He dragged the log into the field. He came back for another piece of tree, and another, until he had cleared a good gap.

"We should be able to get through there," said Pat. He went to get his van . . . but it had gone! Oh! Where could it be? He walked along the road, looking for it. It was parked at the side of the road, next to Sam's mobile-shop.

"I moved your van a bit," said Sam. "I could see your new paint was going to get scratched, with all these branches flying about."

"Thanks, Sam," said Pat. "I'll be on my way now – Peter's managed to clear the road. Cheerio!"

"Cheerio, Pat!"

Peter was moving the last of the logs. Pat waved to him, and called "Thanks, Peter. Cheerio!" as he went through.

"We'll have to get a move on now, Jess," said Pat. But just as he said it, the engine began to make funny noises. "Now what?"

The van jerked, coughed, shook, and stopped.

Pat got out and lifted the bonnet to look at the engine. Just as he was bending over to see better, the wind snatched his hat and blew it along the road.

"Help! My hat!"

It rolled along the road, with Pat chasing after it. It blew over the wall, into the stream, and floated away.

"Oh, no!" said Pat. "I'll never catch it now."

He went back to the van. He mended a broken wire, and soon was on his way again.

There was nobody about at the village school.

"Have they all been blown away?" said Pat. Then he saw the children; they were outside playing in the wind.

But the wind wanted to deliver the letters. It snatched them out of Pat's hand and delivered them in all directions. It blew them across the meadow, behind stones, over walls, and into bushes.

The children helped to find them. One letter was stuck in a tree. Bill Thompson climbed up to get it.

"Careful!" said Pat. "What a day! Hold them tightly, I think they're all *air-letters* today."

Pat blew about the valley all morning, with his letters and parcels. It was almost the end of his windy round, when he saw a flying towel. It was one of Granny Dryden's. He went to help her catch it.

Her washing had blown across the garden and planted itself all over the
place; in the bushes, amongst the roses, on the lawn, behind the shed . . .
everywhere.

"Oh Pat," said Granny Dryden, "this wind's terrible. You are a dear. I'd never
have caught it all by myself. Look, there's more over there."

Pat helped to gather it all in.

"Now we've got my washing," said Granny Dryden, "what about your hat?"

"It blew off miles away," said Pat, "and sailed down a stream."

"Good gracious," said Granny Dryden. "Ted Glen said he'd hooked a post-man's hat out of the lake. I didn't know it was yours. He popped it on the old scarecrow to dry."

There it was, standing in the next field.

"It looks like mine," said Pat, and walked across for a closer look.

"It is mine!"

He took it off the scarecrow and shook out the creases.

"Thanks, Mr. Scarecrow."

Then Pat waved to Granny Dryden.

"Time to blow home," he said. And off he went home to tea, with Jess curled up asleep in his basket.